Coll

ᴄʏ

Norma Powers

ISBN 9798640653021

Norma Powers has had a number of poems published. These include *VINTAGE* which was Commended by Sentinel and *SIR WALTER RALEGH,* which was Highly Commended.
She has published one novel "The Candle House." which was a finalist in a national novel competition. Norma has read her work on local radio in Totnes, and, more recently, at Open Mic readings in Peebles.

Norma Powers was born on the south coast of England. During the Second World War she was evacuated to Wales. After briefly living in Canada and working in advertising copy writing, she returned to England and married. Norma lived for a while in the Far East. She now lives in the Scottish Borders.

Balance

Choosing Words

Connoisseur

Craft

Crocodile

Elephants Bathing

Evacuee

Facing the Past

Feeding the Pigeons

Friday 13th

Frozen Reason

G.S.A

Horses

In the Will

Love

Logic

Mary Madonna

Memories

Mining For You

Mouldiwarps

Potential

Rattle

Safer Ground

Christmas Eve

Seagulls

Sir Walter Raleigh – on his portrait

Spider

Still Life

Survivor

Table Mail

The Colour of Winter

Upwardly Mobile

Values

Water

War Games

Wisdom

Zeitgeist

BALANCE

Beauty can be a bugbear
Loveliness a cheat
Magic is often hard to bear
Awe is a wobbly seat.

Self satisfaction is not appealing
Acceptance may need moderating
Forgiveness brings a hint of healing
Disperses and dilutes the hating.

CHOOSING THE WOMB

Started, hovered, one third formed,
An idea, a wish...
She urged it to come true
For you, and you, and you

But it was not ready
The essence went into the ether
The germ, this more-than-seed
A particle that sought the whole
to cling to. Do flecks remain
In due time to come again?

Is the collective unconscious
Applicable to embryos?
Do articles of faith meld into a whole,
take root and grow?

Are there a limited number of personalities,
Is DNA frugal, recycling into different bodies,
who face the world with memories they cannot have...
and which as childhood fades, fade too.

When a body dies do some genes remain,
To be born again:

A shuffling blind obedience
To imperatives programmed far deeper
Than learning can eradicate or master;
No intellectual searching can prepare

For the long tunnel of death.

And from the birth canal no baby retains its memory
of the journey
Or if it does, then cannot speak of it.

Light is seen the end of the tunnel
and an entity in human form
that scientists state is a physiological symptom
Of death.
Why?
Why should a machine, complex as computers not yet
built
Need this reassurance if there is a total blankness?
It is not a scientific imperative to give spiritual
substance
At the time of death.
It is unnecessary, a fancy, a construct that has no place
In science.

Why should this tunnel
Replicate the birth canal?
There is no need if it is simply physical.

A memory, an imprinting?
And what is the light at the end, and the entity that has
human form?

The spiritual press on us like a tumour
Even in the act of stern denial;

Even in coldest objective intellectualising
There floats a wisp of memory

Elusive as a need
We cannot, we refuse
To justify.

CONNOISSEUR

From opposite directions they collide
on the corner; she swerves sharply, heavy fall of hair
snags on the wall;
in the fading beat of heels
he pauses, slowly peels
four blonde strands
from rough grey stone –
and continues home.

Easing the cork from an ambiguous bottle,
he releases into the still air
only an expensive memory;
the handle of his bedroom door turns
bending the flames from the ivory candle.

Afterwards he winds the strands of stolen hair
around the empty glass's crystal stem,
and he remembers:

…sherry from a plastic glass,
windswept hair blurring his sight;
four hundred thread count sheets
cannot compete with the caress of sand beneath his
feet;
even now the Manzanilla
evokes the salt of her silent tears;

no conquest since
can slake
the unique bitter-sweet memory
of love unsatisfied...

   ...   of love denied.

CRAFT

St Mary's Church
Totnes, Devon

Stone was my skill,

in stone my love lies

as still as stone

and stone is my heart:

petrified.

I dared to love above my station:

a lady betrothed to a lord.

But I was their finest mason,

and valued by the church;

so I received but forty lashes…

They married her in haste to a lesser earl;

my beloved died giving birth to our babe.

I was entrusted to sculpt her form in stone,

and to the chamber of our trysts

in the still of the night, I crept like a thief

to carve her little guardian dog

in bas relief.

CROCODILE

For Barbara – Riverside House

She gazes cross the Tweed,
then down at the stone crocodile
remembering The Nile
where they were the real thing:
reptiles from her nursing days
In Africa.

There is no replica of a camel here,
but one morning as we trek across the terrace,
as she reaches for a handkerchief,
we agree how cold Scottish winds
make ones' eyes water...

I do not think they are
Crocodile tears she sheds.

ELEPHANTS BATHING

Last night was displayed to the sound of trumpets
the ingenuity of man:
he made elephants dance in a sawdust ring:
tinselled giant balance on a stool –
demonstrating that man is a patient skilful -
fool…

But morning brings them swiftly, softly down the
hill,
big and bulky from the circus they come
trunk hooked round tail and tail round trunk
is twelve times curled:
the biggest group of fully trained elephants in the
world.

Sand sinks beneath their feet,
tender tips of trunks search sea air
ears spread like scanners
against the dull grey sky.

They plunge and wallow, leisurely spray.
Then suddenly as if arrested by primal memory
silently they stand -
stopping our hearts.

Black with water, huge in rediscovered pride,

they bellow defiance far and wide.
earning respect and awe
greater than the night before.

EVACUEE

We left home to get away from the bombs;
The country was a foreign place: moles on barbed
wire,
bulls with bayonets on their heads,
and cows whose teeth scissored grass like silk.

At school I found a friend; we did a swap;
my gold bracelet for a whole day
and for me a peach from their tree;
I wore its furry skin
like the gum shield Dad wore in the ring.

At break Mum marched across the playground;
my friend stumbled, pushed up her sleeve,
the safety chain snagged on a darn,
a frantic twist – she thrust it out,
leaving a bangle of blood around her wrist.

When the stone was pockmarked dry
I painted it gold and grandpa
threaded it on fishing twine,
for her to wear around her neck.

Years later when peace came
we hugged goodbye down by the stream,
her cheek felt like a peach against my lips,

but the stone pressed hard against my chest;
we were growing up,
sensing new, forbidden fruit.

*The Aymara people of the Andes, Bolivia believe
the future lies behind us and the past is always ahead.*

FACING THE PAST

Behind the lorry's tailgates the future unrolls
in fumes of our exhaust,
hopes and dreams and future loves
receding…

Our present is here in the lorry's roar,
the sweating, swearing and the laughter,
silenced by thoughts of what comes after.
The distant past was a rabbit, menacing on the
nursery wall,
until we sussed it was a grown-up's fingers –
that's all.

Our rattling, noisy *now* is sheep's wool snagged
on wire,
butterfly dying at our booted feet,
incongruous as sudden longing
for something …

Our future's in imagination, hoisted on our backs:
a gift in a rich rug furled
around a kohl-eyed queen;
behind a veil, or a daddy's girl.
The choice – for now – is ours.

FEEDING THE PIGEONS

She tries never to let them down
and every day
down
they
come...
applauding feathers in free fall
of soft down, to where they sit
she and the old man
with string around his middle.

Their pecking grows jerky
as her long gone wooden toy;
a signal stirs a swirl of sepia, white and grey;
pigeons have lift off into the fading day.

The old man's red rimmed eyes x-ray her paper bag;
she nudges the stuffed egg nearer
and shuffles off
through killer heels, designer bags
and hair as sleek as pigeons' heads;
gowns part around her like The Red Sea,
invisible as Harry Potter in his cloak
she eavesdrops on barristers and lawyers
and debates with herself on what to bring
to the bench tomorrow.

FRIDAY 13TH

The safety handle struck – metal on bone,
there was a crack;
paramedics got you into a chair
with ingenuity
and infinite care.

The upper arm was broken in the worst place
they said, straight-faced:
the humerus.
Railed in the high bed scanning the ward
for the light ahead, came the sound of a grass
cutter;
when the engine cuts out
he is doubtless bound for home
and a home cooked meal,
or maybe a shared micro wave from a bright box.
You try to remember which box you ticked for
supper.

Days when one's arms could lift to bend the
blossom branches
and fingers stroke the silk of petals white and
pink;
but turf now sinks where once you strode
and leaves, once whirled by breezes,
huddle,sullen beside the road.

The right arm learns to operate alone;
the left when not reined in flies out –
hovers jerkily like an arcade crane.
Muscles and tendons free themselves
to grope on fractured bone.
You too seek new support and cling to hope...
which comes in an Xray: shaped like a butterfly;
but this is an incomplete union and like its namesake
It soon dies.

Not Hopper's humans but wise old corvids
are picking out memories
you'd thought to bury deep,
flapping blackly far too close
to eyes that that ache for sleep.

A line of light like a stripper's thigh
appears along the curtain's velvet edge.
Resist the urge to rise'
Pull up the down of duvet,
Shut your ears and eyes
until your doubts become absorbed
Into the blank black nothingness.

Only when the birds of dawn have flown
Can you salvage some green and gold
from the remains of the day.
already growing old.

FROZEN REASON

All is delight, pillow upon pillow piled white,
upon bank and roof
not yet sketched on by claw or paw or hoof;
diamantes glow on black branches where birds
step like women on damp pavements.

The sorbet scrunch of snow under our soles is
soothing …
until we reach the hidden margin where earth
meets water;
bending to touch a shard of ice fingers burn
like a deer's tongue frozen in agony
to a precious salt lick.

Lifting up a sheet of ice – a stench that is almost
feral
rises – invades - .pollutes….
we see now the streaks of grey that mar the virgin
whiteness;
the blue is of veins in aged hands,
or ink diluted by tears;.

With a crack like splintering ice
the air is splintered by the bark
from a distant dog.

Far off in the suddenly alien park

a girl's taunting laugh
is the siren call that has our hands
feeling for the safety mast
of a tree's rough bark.

G.S.A.

Where to place the blame?
On the first explorers, collectors?
More likely planes unloading tourists,
who shed clothes along with inhibitions,
soaking up sun, scattering wild oats.

Two young people standing in front of a cathedral
He is studying the mason's ancient carvings.
Willing this weight of stone to interpose itself between
The images that jerk him awake in the early hours,
His sweating body twisting like those he photographed
On barbed wire in Afghanistan – or was it Iran?

For the last time, going home to a small town in The
Scottish Borders
She too is nearing home and family in the red earthed
soft south-west;
Side by side they face images that have seen it all
before;
Now in this English Autumn, the air between - like a
desert mirage,
blurs their vision.
Choreography directs their hands: one small, pale
sliding
under a fall of light brown hair;
the other broad, tanned, pushes back strands of black
from the faded blue tshirt.

They exchange the smiles of strangers
although they feel they've met before;
and their eyes meet for too long;
They switch to the neutral territory
of platitudes' and honed reactions.
With stunning originality he suggests:
"Gargoyles are great…"
She mocks her own pedantry:
 'Those are Grotesques – the other ones take the
water.'
He gives flourishing mock bow of acknowledgment:
Rare species, she thinks: a male who can stand
corrected.
He focuses his serious camera upward,
While she aims her mobile at him.
Both are stunned by what has hit them;
Until this moment neither has been bound by what
others say
but on that day – that glorious impossible day
something has happened they cannot explain,
though later they keep on trying - try, again and again.
Sex is there, love too, and liking – but there is
something else
neither has faced before.

The coffee is cold by the time they stop talking;
and go their own ways; he north and she south…
Her parents are all hugs and tears and kisses,
they have booked a table at a restaurant: to mark her
coming home;
but her eyes keep zooming in on the fourth chair -
imagining him there.

She shows her photos of beaches and mountains,
Of skyscrapers, and The Statue of Liberty;
But that night she is imprisoned by different pictures
that seem shameful
Here in her single childhood bed.

After three days of phone calls she takes the train
north
to a matter-of-fact grey town
where his vast family is gathered to welcome their boy
home;
names are reeled off and her head is in the whirl of a
ceilidh
whose steps she'll never learn, either.

The next day when they break the news tell of their
intention to marry,
Smiles mark their bewilderment:
 He is home, but home and already they are going to
lose him . –
their youngest too and to matrimony.
Their words are all welcoming – but when they hug
her she seems all bones –
 so small – so pale!

Later they go to Devon armed with photos of his
parents, grandparents
and a scrupulously documented sepia of his family's
history.
Her mum and dad hide their doubts at this whirlwind
romance;

And how can they explain, what they themselves do
not understand?
This is the one.
She'd never dreamed of babies…but now she is…
The wedding is planned…
Probably that winter, no rush they say;
they relish the speculation, the planning…
and bask in the amazement of
having found each other.

They search out photos from their pasts
to form the bedrock of the album they feel necessary
to build
alongside their future's fading emails.
In dusty leather albums in the attic
They point to snapshot details
as artefacts from a lost tribe,
half fearing the riches
of their secret Tutankhamen might perish in the breath
of a relative's unguarded remark.
They delay, prevaricate; delve deeper into yet another
Pandora's box…and find
a box still scented with cigars::
Romeo et Juliette. Perfect …
Here are riches: certificates….of births and marriages
and deaths
crisp in the dust and sun motes of her family attic
where a fly buzzes like distant, receding, gunfire…
easily swatted except …except that it could stain the
memorabilia they painstakingly sift through,
like archaeologists hardly believing the sepia scrawl
on letters,

and the perfect copperplate on certificates of birth, of
marriage and death.

If they had only stopped there.... closed up the
archives,
ended this eager, harmless excavation opened to the air
...
exposed long hidden family history that should have
seen the light long ago
or been sealed up for evermore...
Because they have read too much, checked too much,
and double checked...
And there is no mistake ...

They have never met before: the gargoyles were the
first to see their instant – their unique
recognition that cuts through preamble, flirtation,
straight to the core
GROTESQUE. Yes it is grotesque that a love like
theirs cannot be.
But they are not free
This is one of the last taboos, it is verboten, it is
forbidden by law:
Brother and Sister can love, but not plummet down the
shaft
of lust.

Science can explain succinctly
G.S.A   Genetic   Sexual   Attraction
They are lost, more at sea than any mariner,
for they are committed way beyond imagining,
they are travellers in an antique land

stumbling against the rock of law.

To marry? They search for facts. Is sex forbidden? Too late now...

They do want children, they need to express their love openly, tangibly they want their genes to continue, they long to replicate, bring new individuals into this world.

But no. This cannot be. Their children would face a fate...may inherit traits and disabilities, disfigurements...

Their parents' actions would be stamped, not on a stele, but in the genes, in flesh and blood.

Their 'perfect' love could produce tarnished children.

They cannot bear imagining their children growing up to wish they had never been born....

They refuse to repeat the travesties of history that brought them together, and as their fingers make patterns in the dust, touch each others'cheeks

Their meeting that was such a blessing, such a wonder such a stroke of fate to bring twin souls together ...

They cannot backtrack, cannot deny knowing of these facts.

They will check for any loophole. Is sex forbidden, or just procreation?

The law seems to indicate they can cohabit....but as friends only, as brother and sister...

They groan when they visualise the deceptions, the lies ...

This is the cruellest twist of fate and they curse their family, that continued blithely on, with such lack of imagination ….

Who could have foreseen such a chance encounter…if they had known before….if, for whatever reason, there had been a family gathering, celebration – or funeral – and either of them had planned on coming…..if they had any advance knowledge….

There should have been barbed wire and guards to warn them.

Some deep instinct, primal taboo would have set up barriers, and they would have met as what they are – half brother and sister…

but some fate, in whom they do not believe, set them up…

chance in a million, or twenty million…what are the odds?

Torturing themselves by reading they can find:

The cruellest, the most bitter blow is that such a pull of their specific libido…transcends normal meeting between the sexes.

Flirtations and sizing up are by-passed.   Because their genes recognise each other.   They are twin souls in every way, and forbidden nothing except what they most desire.   Full sexual expression of their love. They are travellers who are lost….

HORSES

Branches splintered, cracked and fell,
gathered, stacked upright to dry;
imagination, skill
sculpted dead wood into horses:
There
      Bare
         Aware
No flesh or muscle, sinew or spleen
to weaken and decay – but distilled force,
standing hugely: h o r s e.

Legs stretch, tails arch,
a stallion's trumpet
blares into the icy wind,
a neighing clarion drowns the tractor's grind,
nostrils flare.
empty orbits see through
our air.

Once upon a future time
the elements will bake their flanks,
split their brittle, flowing tails,
and black confetti drift to earth
around an impotence of hooves …

still thudding
deep into our memories.

IN THE WILL

Death brings them back to the living,
these gifts of stone, of wood or gold,
holding memories of choosing, giving,
ours now to take, to hold.

These gifts of stone, of wood or gold,
like Shabti figures, should be buried deep;
they are not ours to take, to hold...
mute heralds of eternal sleep.

Shabti figures should be buried deep,
not flaunting love's patina in their wear,
unwelcome heralds of eternal sleep,
resurrected to our grudging care,

displaying love's patina. But their wear
holds memories of choosing, giving;
restored to our ungrudging care;
death brings them back to the living.

L O V E

Rose from a crystal goblet,

frothed up to clouds above

edged to the light and sprang into sight

that power which we call love.

Crept through the silver breakers

danced in the shining surf

billowing furling set our heads whirling

came like a star to earth.

Peeped from the tiny fronds

flew from the highest tree

then, twisting lightly, glowing whitely,

united you and me.

LOGIC

He ran with a chestnut filling his cupped palm:
a shiny green mine dropped from a tree.

'Do you know what's in here?'
Tugging me down to his three foot five
'I'll tell you what's in here,' he cried.

Tiny fingers walked the sharp green spines,
indentations fading prints in sand,
'Inside this egg with pins…' he whispered
'Inside, waiting to hatch out –
is a real …live…'

He paused with a showman's flair
wide eyes dared me to deny his logic,
'Inside,' he exploded with a shout
'Is – a – baby –
Hedgehog!'

MARY MADONNA

Stained glass slants its dyes across the altar onto the
stone flags
Rusty, red like her last emissions -
 and the red from bleeding wounds
as He carried the cross to the hill.

She has continued to carry her burden:
the dull and endless knowledge
that she can no more bear a child;
No blood since that day on the hill.
Her son is taken.
And she no longer can conceive another child
to help her heart to heal.
Even if Joseph were not the husk he has become,
she has known,
but her acceptance does not make
the agony less than harrowing.
She is fallow.

Her son is gone.
When they nailed him to the cross
His image came onto her eyes
And will burn there until
they close them for the final time.
Now she inclines her head as once
she bowed to the angel with the news;

Now she mouths again 'thy will be done, and always
thine.'
She was always just the vessel for the wine,
To bear a son who never was hers;
from the day in the temple among the elders
He had made her position cruelly clear:
He went about his heavenly father's business;
the long table was finished by his father -
he knew his place too.
Thy will be done.
Her son is gone.
And if she had again to obey
that awesome command –
knowing what she has learned so hard,
would she hold out her hand
and say she was His to command?
Unworthy as she was?
Oh, no – oh, yes --- maybe …
but one thing Mary knows as her knees
lock in genuflection on the worn church floor
is that she was worthy. She did fulfil all
He asked of her
And more.
So much more.

MEMORIES

I am Rat,
programmed to trap false memories
of our family's past.
Beneath my teeth the jugular
releases life blood,
congealing into impotence.

My claws rake the soft sleek belly
of careful camera poses,
exposing viscera of family hate,
intestines of twisted desire,
and the kidney stench
of stifled resentment.

Indulgence has hardened the arteries,
lungs that struggled to preserve pretence,
and the anguished valves of the heart
are at rest.

The ego's blustering has abated;
Lies are digested,
I rest... sated ...
satisfied.

MINING FOR YOU

I say I love you but you are not here;
you were my nugget and my doubloon
but flake by wafer flake you left the room,
dissolved to where I cannot go.

We sit close but painfully apart,
our memories not matching;
I aim the torch beam of our lives
upon past laughter, even sorrows,
as I pan your errant mind,
where there is no tomorrow.

Although your body is still here,
I learned to accept a widow's mite –
until today; in the public park you think you own,
you hold a daffodil upside down,
raise your face and say:
'The sun's so good.'
Desperate, I sift through my recycle bin
for parties, weddings, christenings
marked by sun, or rain, or hail or wind…

Till down the tunnel of your mind
I glimpse a flickering gleam;

and here beside me on this rusting bench
I do feel it – just.
No counterfeit and no alloy
but the real McCoy
that is you:

Pure

     Gold

         Dust.

MOULDIWARPS

Bodies hang by the mouth on wire,
soft and plump or thin and drier:
tallies of man's skill
to kill.

Computers man the satellite
that ploughs the skies; below the fight
against a mammal small and blind
grinds on.

Man goes to the moon but cannot wipe out
a creature that without a doubt
was programmed by a superior kind
of computer mind.

....

Now Man has given up on the moon
but moles continue doing what they do best -
technology has only changed
the method of their dying.

POTENTIAL

I am your uncalled- for conscience:
the prod behind the elephant's ear.

Once you soared solitary,
eyes raking landscape;
fine- tuning of wings, the pause,
    the focus, the stoop....
        the claws -
           the kill.

But you flew too hard and fast
into the window's glare
and left your dusty negative
impressed there
on domesticity's unyielding glass.

You became a starling hustling for a crust.

We stoop for a peacock feather, an owl's white down,
yet fail to gauge the subtle,
sequinned glow of your sleek plumage.

But when you join your flock,
in soaring synchronicity,
arching like Thai dancers' wrists,

my heart stops, then twists,
to join your plunging flight.

Murmuration lost from sight...

...leaving a new image on my mind:
　superb, and finely etched,
　　indelible,
　　　and re-defined.

RATTLE

A wedding gift, crafted long ago –
symbol of fertility, hope for a new life to be conceived
    tonight or tomorrow,
        a baby's rattle, but also for rejoicing
            and for sorrow.

Designed to gripped in a tiny fist,
  gnawed and gnawed to ease the pain
      in flaming jaws.
                Shaken in frustration
                The high and tinny sounds
    Of the imprisoned bell
    Smothered in yells of

Of practical use no more ….
        Flung too often to the nursery floor
        And brighter challenging toys came along

        Consigned to a biscuit tin with a first tooth,
                bootees, parings from first nails …
        Each minute dent, each piercing of the silver
            As precious as the crabs and Tasmanian tigers
chiselled from hard red rock …
    on an island on the opposite side of the globe
    before the pyramids were conceived…

SAFER GROUND

I should leave,
but your kindness is a spider's web;
swaying in your silk embrace,
words like respect and caring make me feel
confused and - differently –
used.

I learned to move among the panthers
who stalk in sharp suits:
finger on silk tie,
twitch of tail,
assessment in their eyes,
signs I recognise;
and when the lusts of predators
are momentarily sated
I can test the hidden voltage
In the wire around their territory.

But when you stroke my sensitivities
and speak of needs –
my needs – I am
disorientated - not able to grasp
that what you offer
Is far above
and more durable
than love.

CHRISTMAS EVE

They've hemmed me in with Safety & Health;
I can't afford to repair the stable;
the elves are on a slow Go-Slow
It's as much as I'm able to *Ho, Ho, Ho.*
They've issued me sacks of scratchy nylon
That get snarled up in those wretched pylons.
Chimneys are gone, or are far too tight;
Some kids do really need,
But most of their lists are for overpriced tat
To fill an endless, mindless greed.

The final blow's from Arctic Transport:
The noble stags that pull my sleigh
are NOT what they appear:
they shed their antlers at my busiest time of year.
Rudolph?, Prancer? Blitzen?
They're females every single one
bearing their antlers until the spring
when the babies come.

Here's me thinking I was doing good
Driving my team through starry nights
to nice little kids
But it's all as fake, a collosal con
And I'm just a fat old bloke
Who can't appreciate the joke.

SEAGULLS

Descendants of dinosaurs,
free wheeling riders of the clouds,
seeking sustenance from seas,
squawking, white confetti
in the tractor's wake.

We call them vermin,
but we laid waste
to their hunting grounds,
forcing them to scavenge dustbins
and scour our landfill mounds;
now they hustle on café pavements,
raking for protein in discarded batter
innocently gulping down our additives.

They are worthy of admiration,
these entrepreneurs who, under our eyes
filch food from our plates
Before reclaiming the skies.

SIR WALTER RALEGH – On His Portrait

I trusted the artist to do my portrait well:
velvet, lace, brocade he paints with a kitten's tongue
and rapier's accuracy,
But, is my hand, truly so – small?

The Lord knows, and all the court,
that I have wielded sword and fought
many a battle.
So why my effeminate hand?

He has my earring lustrous, my beard in trim,
Pride in the posture, visage grim;
A man who cloaks a puddle
to save the slippers of a queen:
flamboyance spread to stroke her vanity...
But not – oh, not by that weak hand!

He gives no hint of risks I take
in questioning the status quo;
I hold life by a tassel's thread
and there this painter dare not go.
Even our bold virgin queen
will pause before an utterance
as closely as she spies her image in the
looking glass.

He will not dare the perilous waters of the mind
to conquer foreign lands;
for this I lay no blame.

But, oh – it is so poorly done:
that hesitant right hand.

Highly commended by Sentinel Anthology

SPIDER

Minute mimosa ball
spinning silently, softly down your silken thread;
small blob of chrome trapezing, twisting,
you dangle in the spotlight
of the anglepoise upon the desk.

How simple just to press
thumb against forefinger, you in between,
and then release one's fingers nicotined with
ochre dust:
snuff – you - out.

I look up and down you come
pendulum upon the page,
resting marginally:
an eight legged living asterisk.

STILL LIFE

(from a window at Riverside House)

Viewed from the top floor the bird's body
is a composition of ice creams:
vanilla and dark chocolate
moulded neatly, closely.

Where do magpies usually go to die?
One for sorrow seems appropriate.
Two birds would be exaggeration,
three or four an unlikely elation here,
where grandchildren are rare
as magpies' teeth.

Crystals falls on urns and birds of stone,
and on the one of flesh and blood – alone.
A shroud of snow masks plumage and bone,
conceals disintegration.

This little death has pecked from my retina
the lurid dreams of night
and floated them in downstream daylight,
  down and down,
      swirling, and curling ...drowning ....

submerging, surfacing, emerging as
negatives…
or private viewing of a Rothko:
White on black on white.

SURVIVOR

After the nuclear explosion at Hiroshima Japanese women were left with the pattern of the flower from their kimonos on their skin.

Magnolia petals, stuck to the concrete by countless feet;
I bend to retrieve a mouse brown husk,
torn to soon from clenched waxen buds:
rabbit's ears. They twitch me back
to flower power, incense and a poster:
nude blonde with horse on deserted sands.
"She's beautiful," my pupil whispered;
"Not as lovely as you," the platitude slipped out
as smoothly as her zip slid down.
I swept aside the sable of her dead straight hair,
and the image there burned on my retina:
magnolia buds and blossom once on satin
now seared her living skin.

So alive, so full of life was she;
But her gallows humour was disturbing –
I never learned if it survived
From before – *then* – or whether it was etched in acid
– after.

So many questions.   That one I did not dare to ask.

Now, my stiff fingers rub these rabbit's ears and I hear her laughter,

dark as her mocking eyes, as she twists a bare arm,
flaunting her macabre tattoo, needling me.
"Look – I'm dead fashionable. At last.
Cost me a bomb to have it done!"

TABLE MAIL

Not rare or unusual but in pride of place,
framed under glass, hanging on the wall:,
 monetary value nothing at all,
borrowed across the table
 to write across the menu:
                    "Will – you – marry me?

No work of art, just a silver twist- up pencil,
   but its tip keen as an arrow
              propelled
                   us
                     to the altar
                        and, sixty years
                        down
                            the line,
                               we're doing fine.

THE COLOUR OF WINTER

Red is the colour of winter:

fat waxen globes of tulips beckon from a window;
a fleecy flaunts its poppy optimism
among the coats of black and brown;
the snowman's scarf is always a circle of cherry.

Tweedledum and Tweedledee
united in their livery of pillar box red;
wait with gaping mouths
to swallow our season's greeting cards.

A bag of Hula Hoops whoops it up
along a pewter pavement;
high in a leafless tree the robin competes
with the russet of a woolly glove
snatched by the wind and caught by a branch.

A billion vermillion berries invite the birds
to peck, swallow, digest, and drop
next year's crop beneath the snow.

UPWARDLY MOBILE

The clematis and thornless yellow rose
rooted happily in the kitchen bed,
tenacious baby tendrils
curled among the trellis;
white flowers trailed their fugitive scent,
across the window vent.

The climbing partners dug their crampons deep,
spread themselves across our bungalow wall,
in search of a grander home.

We tried cutting them down to size,
persuasion: snipping, twisting and tying in
with softest string;
but they moved beyond our control
searching for their destinies
on towering, mellow ancient stone.

We've called a truce;
now they hang loose.
Dainty roses of chrome
enhance our - slightly darker - room
and Flammula's white stars
haunt the air with her classy perfume.

VALUES

Too late to rescue my precious ring as it swirls

down the plug hole in a tangled curl of hair;

but a pearl is only an oyster's reject …

and life is not an S-bend…

…is it?

VINTAGE

Above my head the trapdoor holds at bay
their jargon; their claptrap traps me here
to study spiders, watch a dilute sun
slip over iron bands on wooden casks;
my tears are private esters, not depression
but a complex distillation -
vintage melancholia.

Save me from experts who talk of closure.
I am a champagne bottle: my wire cage
criss-crosses the dusty window high above,
each remouage stirs my soul.
But mystery is not eased out like a cork.
I choose to sit and mull,
recall past scents that linger in my skull.

I am not crying, merely anticipating dying,
I do not want the kindness of their lies,
only a casual touch for its own kind's sake,
and an acid word or two to help
their patronage go down.

Decant me like an ancient bottle;
ease out the cork
and let me settle...
p le a s e.

published in Sentinel Magazine

WATER

You say you love me for myself,
What part is that? My body?
Risky, risky.
All of me, why not take all of me?'
Or two thirds say …65% to 67%
I'll flow through your fingers – heaven sent.

I'll be your refuge and your deluge
'*Water, water, everywhere,*
and not a drop to drink.'

Drink to me only with thine eyes,'
Let's rhapsodise together,
side by side in all kinds of weather.

Water, water, water, love me like you oughta,
water's good for us except ---knock knock on wood:
Too little - oops, too bad,
Too much, uh, huh, not good.

Are you on fire for my stimulating brain?
Think again: three quarter's water!

H_2O is what I am. H_2O and HO, HO, HO,
Have to laugh or I'd cry,
We have one thing in common:
Water, water till we die.

H_2O… HO, HO, HO,
So come on, darlin'

Let's go
        GO
            GO!!

WAR GAMES

Footsteps heavy on the stairs, key grates in lock;
I sweep the tiny armies off the table,
French and English all mixed up.

My two messengers come in,
collars turned up like Aventails –
not quite hiding their wobbly chins.

'Your great grandpa's gone.'

Water sounds like Niagara into the kettle;
mini sand bags of tea in our mugs,
as we drink in silence, hands groping, gripping.

Last week great gramps was helping me paint Zulu
warriors
but when the brush fell from his gnarly fingers
he'd stomped outside
to swear angrily into his white roses.

Yesterday, high up on a gurney he'd gripped my hand,
and he'd grinned
'Reckon this is my last operation, son.'

Now he's lost his last battle,
And the war.

I rescue the Duke from a tissue on the floor:

sodden and crumpled like a white rose;
Will they let Wellington and our Sergeant
be buried together?
And – just this once he won't mind me picking a white
rose
to throw on his grave…
Will he?

Mum is hiccupping sobs, laughing,
and shaking her head:
'This tea's like cats' pee'.
Yes. 'Cats' pee'.   That's what he said.'

WISDOM

Understanding does not come
always as an old man home,
slowly, at the end of day,
careful, ironic, wise and grey.

A golden child may flood with light
your room of ignorance – hold tight
to her swift youth and recognise
that wisdom comes in any guise.

ZEITGEIST

It's in the air, a groping smoky antidote to practicality.
The Dressing Table

Once we sat to use the pots and tubes
we hoped would hold at bay
the future glimpsed in a loved one's image
behind our shoulder.

But we shed this anachronism, this space consumer,
and did our faces standing, which was fine ...until
Dissatisfaction sent us scouring charity shops
to reclaim our former rejects.
A mahogany table, drawers lined with old news
revealed a heavy old penny;
pale utility, its logo like a shingled flapper;
a gilded table boasting blowsy roses and simpering
putti
with broken noses;
a deal table stained with old slap, its frame of empty
sockets waiting
for their long-life bulbs to light a mini stage;
and, of course, the kidney shape with clinking rings for
frilly curtains.

Then entered the mirrors.
a speckled oval sends a silvery reflection;

an austere black rectangle with blanks that once held
prints
of impossibly pretty countryside;
and one vast round mirror supported like a child on a
swing;
by two small acolytes, revealing in our eyes

Sanctuary,

Surprise,

Self consciousness.

.

Printed in Great Britain
by Amazon

16415528R00048